Barbie
W9-CEA-075

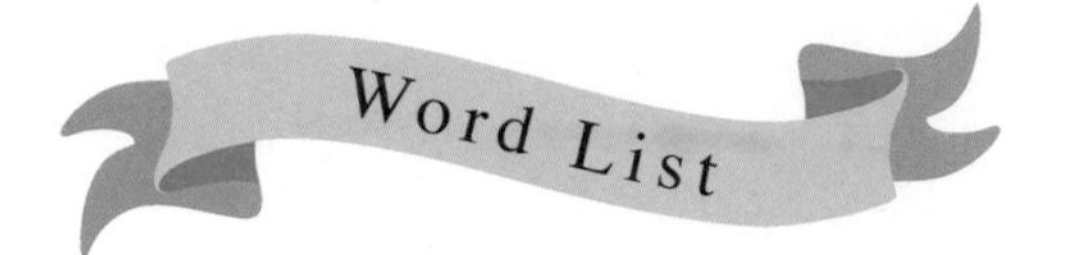

Here is a list of words that might make it easier to read this book. You'll find them in boldface the first time they appear in the story.

gymnastics	jim-NAS-ticks
invitations	in-vuh-TAY-shuns
miserable	MI-zer-buhl
scavenger	SKA-vuhn-jer
appreciate	uh-PREE-shee-ayt
gentlest	JENT-lest
hayloft	HAY-lawft
barbecue	BAR-bi-kyoo
decorations	de-kuh-RAY-shunz
caravan	KAIR-uh-van
confetti	kuhn-FE-tee

Barbie™

Published by Grolier Books, a division of Grolier Enterprises, Inc.
Story by Claire Jordan. Photo crew: Scott Fujikawa, Shirley Ushirogata, Tim Geisen, Rob Holley, Lisa Collins, and Judy Tsuno.
Produced by Bumpy Slide Books.
Printed in the United States of America.
ISBN: 0-7172-8892-7

Gym Tastic
HAPPY BIRTHDAY

Stacie turned a perfect cartwheel. “That was a fun party!” she called to her friend Janet. The two girls were waiting for their ride outside the **gymnastics** studio.

“The best,” agreed Janet, who was upside down doing a headstand. Stacie hurried over to hold her friend’s feet steady.

Stacie was turning another cartwheel when she spotted her sister’s blue van pulling into the parking lot. “Here’s Barbie,” she said. The two girls grabbed their gym bags and raced to the car.

“How was the party?” Barbie asked the

girls as they buckled their seat belts.

"Great!" Stacie replied. "They had gymnastics instructors there to teach us all sorts of cool moves."

"And we got to do our own floor routines," Janet added.

"And we got to use the trampoline," Stacie cut in.

Barbie laughed. "Whoa! One at a time!"

The girls continued talking about Erin's ninth birthday party. Erin's parents had invited everyone in Stacie's class to Gym-Tastic, the children's gymnastics studio. At the party, all the kids got to use the equipment as much as they wanted. Instructors showed them how to put a floor routine to music. Then, at the very end, the instructors performed routines of their own.

"You should have seen them, Sis!" exclaimed Stacie. "They were awesome!"

As they rode along, Janet turned to her friend and said, "Your birthday is coming up soon, Stace.

Where are you going to have your party?"

Stacie peered around the front seat. Barbie didn't seem to be listening. She was humming along to the radio. Stacie whispered back, "My sisters are trying to keep it a surprise, so I don't know for sure. But I think it might be at On Stage."

"I've never heard of On Stage," Janet replied.

"It's new," Stacie explained. "They have a stage, costumes, lights, and music. You decide what kind of show you want to put on. You pick out the parts you want everyone to play. Then everybody puts on costumes and rehearses. When your parents come to pick you up, they get to watch your show! It's like being a real actor!"

As Stacie spoke, she saw Barbie glance in the rearview mirror and smile. Had she heard them talking about On Stage? Maybe Barbie's smile meant that she was right about plans for an On Stage party! Stacie almost asked her right then, but she knew her sisters wanted to surprise her.

"Wow!" Janet cried. "That would be even better than Erin's party."

Stacie couldn't help but grin.

Soon Barbie pulled the van into Janet's driveway.

"Call me tonight if you find out anything," Janet whispered to Stacie. "Thanks for the ride, Barbie," she said louder so Barbie could hear.

"Say 'hi' to your mom for me," Barbie called.

"I will," Janet replied, closing the door.

Stacie settled back in her seat and thought about On Stage. Finally she couldn't stand it any longer. "Sis, you have to tell me where my party is going to be. *Please?*" Stacie pleaded.

Barbie laughed. "Absolutely not!"

"Then will you at least give me a hint? Please, please, *please?*" begged Stacie.

"It will be just as much fun as Erin's was," Barbie told her, smiling. "You'll have a good time, and so will your friends."

"That's not much of a hint," Stacie grumbled, crossing her arms over her chest. Stacie wished her sister would tell her. She wanted to plan her show. But Barbie didn't say another word about it.

After dinner, Stacie spoke to Janet on the phone. "Why don't you ask Skipper?" Janet said.

"I guess I could try," Stacie agreed. But she was pretty sure that her teenage sister wouldn't give away any secrets. After hanging up the phone, Stacie ran downstairs. She was just about to holler for Skipper when she heard voices in the kitchen. She froze in her tracks and listened. She heard Barbie say the word *party,* and her heart began to race with excitement. They must be talking about her birthday party! She tiptoed toward the kitchen.

Finally she heard Skipper say the word *play*. It was true! The party would be at On Stage! Stacie couldn't help it. She started jumping up and down in the hallway.

Just then, Barbie called, "Stace, is that you?"

Stacie realized she had to stay calm. She entered the kitchen and said "hi" to her sisters. She strolled over to the refrigerator and poured herself a glass of milk. Then she popped a chocolate chip cookie into her mouth and chewed it slowly.

Skipper stood up and said, "Well, I have some homework to finish. I'll see you two later."

Barbie turned to Stacie. "Is anything exciting happening at school this week?" she asked.

"Well, not at *school,"* Stacie answered with a wink. She wanted to let Barbie know she was in on the secret. Stacie was sure that her sister would ask if she had overheard the party plans.

Instead, Barbie replied, "Really? What's up?"

Stacie smiled. She would keep the secret, too. "Oh, I'll tell you later," she teased. She finished her milk and ran upstairs. She grabbed the phone and dialed Janet's number.

"Janet!" Stacie whispered into the receiver. "I was right! My party *is* going to be at On Stage!"

Stacie dreamed about her On Stage party that night. And she thought about it the next morning. In the middle of getting dressed for school, she plopped down on her bed and stared into her closet. She tried to imagine what kind of clothes they would have at On Stage. There, she could wear whatever costume she wanted.

"Hmmm," Stacie wondered out loud, "shall I be the cowgirl or the warrior princess today? Since it's Monday—"

"Stacie!" Barbie called up the stairs. "You just missed your bus! Now I'll have to drive you to school. Hurry up!"

Stacie jumped up and threw on some clothes. She grabbed her backpack and ran downstairs. Barbie handed her a piece of toast with peanut butter as they rushed out the door.

"What were you doing?" Barbie asked her little sister. "It was so quiet up there, I thought you had fallen back to sleep."

Stacie was embarrassed. "I'm sorry, Barbie."

As soon as Barbie dropped her off, Stacie could tell that something big was going on at school. Kids from her third-grade class were huddled outside in groups, talking excitedly. Stacie was just about to ask her friend Katie what was going on when Erin ran up to her.

"Janet just told us all about your party," Erin cried. "Your sisters are so cool!"

Before Stacie could say anything, Janet was by her side. "Sorry, Stace," her friend began. "I just told one or two people. Then before I knew it, the whole class found out."

Stacie realized that she probably shouldn't have told *anyone* about her party until she knew for sure. Still, she really liked how it felt to be the center of attention.

"That's okay," Stacie told Janet. "They would have found out anyway when I passed out the **invitations.**" She wondered what kind of invitations she would have. Maybe they would be in the shape of a theater ticket.

"When are you handing them out?" Katie asked from behind her.

"I'm not sure," Stacie admitted. Then she added quietly, "I'm not even supposed to know about the party yet."

When the bell rang, the students hurried to their classrooms and found their seats. But instead of following the lesson, Stacie flipped open her notebook to the calendar page. Her birthday was on a Wednesday, so the party would probably be the Saturday before or after it.

Suddenly Stacie heard someone cough. When she turned around, her friend Janet dropped a piece of paper on the floor. Stacie looked around. Mrs. Brown, their teacher, was checking someone's homework. Stacie leaned over and picked up the note. She gasped as she read it.

Just then, Mrs. Brown looked up. She walked down the aisle to Stacie's desk and saw the note.

"Stacie," her teacher said in a stern voice, "you know the rules about passing notes. Please share it with the class."

Miserable, Stacie stood up. She felt her face turn bright red. It was bad enough to be caught passing notes. But having to read *this* one out loud was worse. Stacie sighed and read, "Todd is having his birthday party at AquaSplash Water Park! It's going to be the best birthday party ever!"

Everyone began talking at once. AquaSplash

Park! It had a wave pool, water slides, paddleboats, and tubes for floating.

"All right, class!" Mrs. Brown called. "That's enough. You can sit down, Stacie. Now that we have had our morning news, let's go on to math. Yesterday we talked about . . ."

Mrs. Brown's voice faded as Stacie stared at the note. She could still hear kids around her whispering about Todd's party. "That's okay," she thought. "Let him have his AquaSplash party. Mine is still going to be better."

But Stacie's day only seemed to get worse. During math, she realized she'd spent so much time thinking about her party that she had forgotten to do her homework. Now, whenever the class came to a difficult question, Mrs. Brown always seemed to call on her. Katie and Janet tried to help by raising their hands, but it was no use. Finally Stacie had to admit that she hadn't done her homework. Her teacher immediately wrote it down in her grade book.

At gym, Stacie thought her day might get better. Her gym teacher announced that they would be playing her favorite game, dodgeball. Everyone knew Stacie was great at dodgeball, so she was picked first for one of the teams. But for some reason, Stacie got tagged at the start of every game. So she had to sit in the bleachers until each game was over. Stacie couldn't figure it out. She began to wonder if everyone on the other team was after her.

At lunchtime, Stacie decided not to sit with her friends at their usual table. Instead she quickly ate her lunch in class and slipped away to the library. She didn't want to see anyone. Stacie pretended to read until it was time to go back to class. At the end of the day, though, she couldn't avoid her classmates any longer. Todd and Erin sat together on the bus, talking about Todd's party. Stacie didn't say a word.

It was as if no one had even heard about her On Stage party. It didn't seem to matter to anyone anymore. Stacie felt tears burning in her eyes. She blinked them away and looked down at her math book. Her party would be boring compared to Todd's. How could anything top a water-park party?

Finally Todd asked, "Stace, what's wrong? Your party isn't the same day as mine, is it?"

"I don't know exactly when my party is," Stacie explained again. "I'll have to check." She didn't want them to know how she really felt—that she didn't like Todd getting all the attention.

"Well, find out today, if you can," said Erin.

Stacie forced herself to smile. "I'll try," she replied, getting off the bus.

Barbie was in the backyard, reading the newspaper, when Stacie got home. Their baby sister, Kelly, was playing in her sandbox. Barbie laid down the paper and asked, "How was school?"

Stacie didn't answer for a moment. The newspaper was open to a full-page ad for FunWay Park! Stacie looked at the ad and then at Barbie. "I'm sorry. What did you say?" she asked.

"I was wondering how school was," Barbie repeated. Then she followed her sister's gaze. "But I think you're more interested in this amusement park. It sure looks like a great place."

Stacie nodded excitedly. "It is! They have the best rides there. My favorite is the one that flips you upside down. It's so scary, you just scream

FUN WAY
PARK

your head off. It's awesome!"

Barbie laughed.

Then Stacie remembered Todd's party. "We found out today that Todd is having his party at AquaSplash Park," she said sadly.

"That should be fun," Barbie replied. She picked up her date book. "When is his party?"

Just as Stacie began to tell her, they heard the front door slam.

"Barbie, I'm home!" Skipper called through the house. "I checked about rides for the party and—" When she saw Stacie, she stopped talking.

Stacie looked from one sister to the other, then back at the newspaper. Rides? The party? FunWay Park! Then, to her older sisters' surprise, Stacie gave them each a big hug and raced inside.

Stacie quickly dialed her friend's number. "Janet!" she said breathlessly. "Guess what? My party isn't going to be at On Stage after all. It's going to be at FunWay Park!"

Stacie explained to Janet about Skipper's slipup. "My sisters must be deciding all the rides we can go on."

"They sure are tricky," Janet laughed. "This is turning into a fun year for parties."

Todd agreed when he heard about the party the next day. "Hey, Stace," he said, "why don't you see if your sisters have set a date for your party? If they haven't, maybe you could have yours the day after mine. That way, everybody could go to AquaSplash one day and FunWay Park the next."

"That's a great idea!" Stacie agreed.

By lunchtime everyone in her class was buzzing about the double-party weekend. They crowded around Stacie and Todd, who listened as everyone shouted out all the rides they would go on. One girl suggested that they have water-slide races at AquaSplash. One of the boys suggested that they have a **scavenger** hunt at FunWay Park. Stacie wrote down all their suggestions. She couldn't wait to tell Barbie and Skipper about all the ideas. This really would be the best birthday party ever!

Stacie ran into the house that afternoon. "Hey, everybody!" she shouted.

"What is it?" her oldest sister called, hurrying into the living room. Barbie looked around, worried that something was wrong. Skipper came in from the kitchen. Kelly followed her. The two-year-old was carrying her favorite toy, an old stuffed cat named Cookie.

Then Stacie remembered. She wasn't supposed to know about her party. Still, she wanted to make sure that they could have it the day after Todd's.

"Well," Stacie began thoughtfully, "I know it's supposed to be a surprise. But I know about my party."

"You do?" Barbie asked.

"Oh, no, I *did* give it away!" Skipper cried. "I should have made sure you weren't home yesterday before I said anything."

"Well, it wasn't just that," Stacie added. "Barbie sort of gave me a hint, too."

Barbie looked confused. "I did?"

Stacie smiled. "You were looking at the newspaper yesterday," she explained. "I saw the ad."

Barbie looked even more confused, so Stacie continued. "It's a good thing, though. Now that I know, we can plan my party for the day after Todd's. It'll be twice the fun."

Barbie thought for a moment. "Well, that would be a nice idea," she agreed. "But are you sure you don't want your party to be on a different weekend?"

"Yes," Skipper added, "it would make your weekend more special."

Stacie shook her head. "With my party at FunWay Park, and Todd's at AquaSplash Park, we *should* have them the same weekend. It'll be an all-fun weekend. Everybody in my class is excited about it!" Then Stacie pulled out her notes. "I have all kinds of ideas for the party."

Barbie and Skipper looked at each other with their mouths open.

"I know it was supposed to be a surprise," Stacie said again quickly. "It's just that, since I'm having my party at FunWay—"

"Stace," Barbie finally interrupted, "I think there's been a mistake." Barbie looked at Skipper and sighed. She turned back to Stacie. "Your party isn't going to be at FunWay Park."

Now it was Stacie's turn to be confused. Were they having the party at On Stage after all?

"So, it will be a play party, at On Stage," Stacie stated. "I heard you say something about a play the other day," she told Skipper.

Skipper shook her head. "No, the party's not at On Stage, either," she explained. Then she smiled. "It's going to be at Jessie's farm!"

Jessie was a good friend of the family. She was like an aunt to Stacie. Stacie would spend a couple of weeks there every summer visiting and helping out.

Stacie stared at Barbie and Skipper. "My party is going to be on a *farm?*"

Barbie nodded. "You've had so much fun visiting there every summer. Skipper thought your friends would like it, too."

"Won't that be great?" Skipper asked excitedly.

"But . . . but you talked about a play and rides," Stacie said to Skipper.

"I was talking about games to play," Skipper explained. "I even asked Jessie if you and your friends could ride her horse, Whispy."

"Horsie!" Kelly cried, clapping her hands.

"Jessie's really excited about the party," Barbie added.

"Well, I'm not," Stacie blurted out. "Games? On a farm? That's baby stuff! It'll be the most boring party ever!" She knew she should stop, but she couldn't. She had to make her sisters understand. "My friends won't come. Besides, who wants to open presents in a barn?"

"Stacie—" Barbie began.

Stacie interrupted her. "We *have* to have the party at FunWay," she demanded. "Everyone in my class thinks it's going to be there."

It took all of Stacie's strength to hold back her tears. She stared at her teenage sister, whose face was bright red. "Skipper's upset about it, too," Stacie thought. "*She* understands what I mean. She'll tell Barbie to change the party."

Finally Skipper spoke. "Fine!" she snapped. "Have your party at some dumb park. See if I care!" Then she spun around and stomped upstairs.

Shocked, Stacie turned to her oldest sister. "What's Skipper so upset about?" she wondered out loud. "After all, it's *my* party."

"That's true, Stacie. But it was *Skipper's* idea," Barbie replied. "She has been planning the whole thing."

Stacie looked at her feet. She was embarrassed and confused. She didn't want to hurt Skipper's feelings. But she didn't want to have her party on a farm, either. She sighed. "It's just . . . what will I tell Janet, Todd, and everybody else tomorrow?"

The thought of school made Stacie feel just awful. For the second time, she would have to tell everyone that she had been wrong about her party.

Even worse, she would have to tell them that it wasn't going to be a FunWay party. It was going to be a farm party!

Stacie frowned at Barbie. "This isn't fair," she stated. "You tricked me. I never would have told anybody I was having the party at On Stage or FunWay if you hadn't made me think that!"

"Stacie," Barbie said sternly, "we did *not* trick you. We never told you that the party would be at either place. You heard and saw some things. And you misunderstood what they meant. Your party was always going to be at Jessie's farm."

Stacie knew that Barbie was right. Barbie and Skipper had never told her where the party would be. She had nobody to blame but herself. Still, Barbie could fix things. She and Skipper could move the party to FunWay Park. But Stacie knew they wouldn't.

"You are the meanest sister in the world!"

Stacie shouted and ran up to her room. She slammed her door so hard that the glass unicorn on her desk fell over and broke. Stacie burst into tears. She buried her head in her pillow and cried.

She waited for her sisters to come upstairs and tell her that they had changed their minds. She could have her party at FunWay Park after all. Stacie fell asleep, waiting and wishing for those words.

Chapter Four

A ringing sound woke Stacie. She blinked and looked around. The glowing numbers on her clock said 7:30. She rubbed her eyes and got up to get ready for school. As she opened her door, the ringing stopped. Stacie heard Barbie answer the phone downstairs.

"I'm sorry, Katie," Barbie said. "Stacie can't come to the phone right now."

Stacie was about to call down that she was awake. Then she looked out the window. It wasn't morning at all. It was night. Stacie rubbed her eyes again. They were puffy and sore. Then she remembered: The farm party, and the awful things she had said to her sisters. Stacie wanted to cry all over again, but she didn't have any tears left. Instead she sat down on the top stair and rested her head on her knees.

"Thanks, Katie," Barbie said into the phone. "We just want Stacie to have a fun party. I'm sure she'll tell you about our plans tomorrow. Good-bye."

"That was Katie," Stacie heard Barbie tell Skipper. "She said that you and I are great sisters for planning such a cool party for Stacie at FunWay Park."

"Wait until she hears it's on a farm," Skipper replied.

Stacie lifted her head. Skipper sounded so angry and hurt.

"I just thought it would be such a fun idea," Skipper continued. "Stacie loves that farm. I thought it would give her a chance to show her friends all around. They could do all the things Stacie likes to do there: They could ride Whispy, go for a hayride, milk the cows, and even go swimming, if they wanted to. And Jessie said she has some chicks due to hatch that week." Skipper sighed again. "But I guess Stacie's getting too old for that sort of thing."

Stacie listened. Did this mean her party might still be at FunWay Park?

"Skipper," Barbie began, "it *is* a fun idea. Stacie is getting older, but she still has a lot of growing up to do. Right now, she's only thinking of herself. I hope she'll think about how much work you've put into this."

"She's acting pretty selfish," Skipper agreed. "But it *is* her birthday. I want her to be happy. Maybe we should just have the party at FunWay, even though it's so much more expensive."

"Let's talk about it tomorrow," Barbie suggested. "We're all too upset to really think clearly about it tonight."

Stacie crept back to her room. Barbie had said they would talk tomorrow. There was still a chance. But then Stacie thought about all the trouble Skipper had gone to already. For some reason, having the party at FunWay Park didn't seem like so much fun anymore.

Stacie changed into her pajamas. She hadn't eaten dinner, but she didn't feel hungry. She just wanted to go to bed. If she could sleep, she could forget about the whole day. Stacie closed her eyes. She turned onto her side. She rolled onto her back. She pushed her stuffed animals away from her. She pulled them back. Finally Stacie sat up. It was no use. She couldn't sleep. She heard Barbie go into her room next door.

Stacie tiptoed to Barbie's room and knocked

softly. Barbie invited her in. "I couldn't sleep," Stacie said, opening the door.

"Sit down, Stace," Barbie told her. "I'll be back in a minute." She came back with a wet washcloth. "Here, put this over your eyes," she said gently.

Stacie did as Barbie suggested. The cool, wet washcloth made her swollen eyes feel better. "I'm sorry about what I said," Stacie began. "I was just really upset. And I'm worried about what my friends are going to think."

"Skipper was worried about that, too," Barbie pointed out. "More than that, she was worried about what *you* thought. She was trying to do something nice for you. She's hurt that you don't seem to **appreciate** all the work she's put into your party."

Stacie set down the washcloth. "I don't want to face my friends, Barbie. First I told everybody that the party was at On Stage. Then

I told them it was at FunWay Park. That was okay because FunWay is even better than On Stage. But now . . ." Stacie couldn't finish. No matter how she said it, she would sound mean and selfish. A farm party just wouldn't sound as exciting as a party at FunWay.

"Stacie," Barbie explained, "friends should want to come to your party because they like you, not because of where you have it. If that's all they care about, you have to decide whether they are really your friends. A *real* friend cares about you." She looked at Stacie. "It's the same way with sisters."

Stacie smiled and gave Barbie a hug. "You're right. I'm sorry for the way I behaved. I guess I've been acting pretty spoiled."

Barbie smiled and nodded.

"And I'm going to make it up to Skipper," Stacie added. "I promise."

Stacie said good night and put the washcloth

back in the bathroom. Skipper's door was closed. Stacie thought about knocking. Instead, she went back to her room. She picked up her glass unicorn. It had only broken into two pieces. She could fix it. Stacie just hoped that tomorrow she could fix things with Skipper.

The next morning, Stacie was the first one downstairs. She set the table for breakfast and put out the cereal and milk. When Skipper came downstairs for breakfast, Stacie smiled and said, "Good morning."

Skipper just looked at her younger sister and said nothing.

Stacie took a deep breath. "Skip," she began, "I'm really sorry for all the awful things I said. I know you have put a lot of work into my party. It will be fun. None of my friends has ever been on a farm before."

"Are you sure?" Skipper asked softly. "I've been thinking. If you really had your heart set on

FunWay, we could try—"

Stacie put up her hand and shook her head. "That's okay, thanks." She swallowed hard. "Do you have the invitations ready?" she asked. Stacie wasn't sure if she felt brave enough to give them out today. But she knew that it would help Skipper feel better if she asked.

Skipper took the invitations out of a drawer. "You're sure?" she asked again.

Stacie really *wasn't* sure, but she said, "Of course. And I want everybody to have an invitation today so they will know the date." She put the invitations into her backpack.

As Skipper ate breakfast, Stacie went upstairs. She knew if she took long enough brushing her teeth and fixing her hair, Barbie would have to drive her to school. Then she wouldn't have to sit near Todd on the bus. And she wouldn't have to tell him about her party.

Her plan worked. Barbie dropped Stacie off

at school just a minute before the bell rang. Stacie took a deep breath. "Here goes," she thought. She concentrated on her lessons. Once, when she looked up, Stacie saw Todd signaling to her. Stacie smiled at him. Then she looked back at her social-studies book. At lunchtime, though, Stacie couldn't avoid Todd any longer.

"What did your sisters say?" Todd asked, coming over to her table.

Janet and Katie came up behind him.

"Can we have the two parties back to back?" Janet wanted to know.

"Well," Stacie said, pushing her potato puffs around her plate, "my party isn't going to be at FunWay after all."

"Oh," Katie replied. "So it's going to be at On Stage?"

Stacie shook her head and stuffed a forkful of potato puffs into her mouth. It gave her a moment to think.

"They changed their minds again?" asked Todd.

Stacie swallowed. "No, that was my fault. I thought they were planning a party at those places, but they weren't." She was afraid to look at her friends.

"So, where is the party going to be?" Janet wondered.

Stacie felt smaller and smaller. She cleared her throat. "Our friend Jessie has a farm, and that's where it's going to be," Stacie finally blurted out. There. Now they knew. Stacie braced herself. What if they laughed?

"A farm?" Todd repeated. "Hey, that's different."

Stacie slowly pulled out the invitations. "I know it's not FunWay Park or On Stage," she apologized, "but it should be fun. I've spent a lot of summers at the farm. There's a creek for swimming, and Jessie has horses, too. She said we could ride Whispy, her prettiest, **gentlest** horse."

"I love horses!" Janet exclaimed.

"I remember you talking about Jessie's farm," Katie pointed out. "It always sounded like a lot of fun."

"Do they have a **hayloft** there?" Todd asked. "My dad grew up on a farm. He said that he and my uncles used to climb up a ladder to the hayloft. Then they'd swing down on a rope. I've always wanted to do that."

Relieved, Stacie smiled at her friends. "Do you think it'll be okay with everybody else? I know I got them all excited about On Stage and FunWay. I hope they won't be disappointed."

"Well, there's only one way to find out," Janet replied. She pointed to the stack of invitations in Stacie's hand.

Janet was right. Stacie hurried around the lunchroom. She handed out invitations, saying,

"Hope you can come." Before anyone could ask her about the change in plans, the bell rang. As she walked back to class, Stacie heard someone behind her say, "A farm? I thought it was going to be at FunWay Park."

Stacie hurried through the crowd so that she wouldn't have to hear any more. "No matter who comes," she thought, "*I'm* going to have a good time . . . right?"

Chapter Five

"I'm home!" Stacie called. She found her sisters in the backyard again. "I gave out all the invitations," she announced.

"Any answers yet?" Skipper asked.

Stacie wasn't sure how to answer. "Katie, Janet, and Todd are really excited," she replied truthfully. "The other kids have to check with their parents, I guess. They'll call to let us know." Skipper looked a little worried, so Stacie added, "But I bet everybody will come!"

Barbie smiled. "We were just getting ready to go shopping for your party. We thought we'd have a **barbecue** with chicken, corn on the cob, and then birthday cake. How does that sound?"

"Great!" Stacie answered. Just then she had an idea. "Can I come shopping, too?" she asked.

"Of course!" Barbie told her.

Stacie ran upstairs and grabbed some money from her piggy bank. In a flash, she was ready.

Shopping for the party was fun. Stacie helped choose the party favors and goodies for the treat bags. While Barbie and Skipper ordered the cake, Stacie sneaked away and bought a few things on her own.

When they got home, Stacie helped put the party things away. Skipper asked if she wanted to talk about **decorations** for the party. Stacie shook her head. "Uh, I have some things I need to do," she said and hurried to her room.

BREAD

From behind her closed door, Stacie listened for the phone. No one called. Then there was a knock at her door. "Stace?" Barbie called. "May I come in?"

"Just a minute!" Stacie replied. She quickly stuffed her secret project under her bed. Then she opened the door.

"I just wanted to make sure you're okay," Barbie explained. "You've really made Skipper happy. But are you still worried about the party?"

Stacie wanted to say no, but she couldn't. "What if nobody comes?" she whispered. "Skipper will be so disappointed."

"What about you?" Barbie asked.

"Oh, I'm okay," Stacie replied. "I'm pretty sure Katie, Janet, and Todd are coming. Even if nobody else comes, we'll have a good time."

"I think it's too soon to worry about it," said Barbie. "The party is still a week away. People will call. Besides, you're happy, and Skipper's happy. So I'd say this party is already a success."

The next day, Janet and Katie told Stacie they would come to the party. Todd, Cindy, and Erin also said they would be there. When Stacie got home, Barbie had messages from the parents of Stacie's other friends, too. Even Whitney would try to come. Stacie made a list.

"That's about half the class," Stacie told Barbie and Skipper. "That's a good number."

When they were finished with dinner, Stacie excused herself and went to her room. As she climbed the steps, she overheard Skipper ask Barbie, "Is Stacie okay? She's been spending an awful lot of time in her room. Do you think she's still worried about the party?"

Stacie paused and listened.

"I don't know," Barbie answered. "Whatever it is, though, I think we should let her work it out. It's like you said, Skipper, Stacie is getting older. I'm sure she can handle it."

Stacie smiled and continued up the stairs.

The day of the party was bright and sunny. Stacie, Barbie, and Skipper loaded the van with party supplies. Stacie could hardly wait to get to the farm. When they arrived, Barbie and Jessie took Kelly to see the baby chicks. Stacie raced Skipper to the barn and swept the floor. They strung twinkle lights along the rafters. As Stacie looked down from the hayloft, she remembered what Todd had said about swinging down from it. She knew that Jessie wouldn't want kids dropping down from the hayloft. But what about dropping balloons?

"Hey, Skip!" Stacie called. "I have an idea!"

Stacie and Skipper borrowed some netting from Jessie. They strung it across the hayloft and let four long ribbons dangle down. Then they opened a bag of balloons and began blowing them up. As fast as they could fill the balloons, Barbie and Jessie put them in the netting.

Stacie was having so much fun that she forgot to watch the time. When they were done with the balloon net, it was already half an hour after the party was supposed to begin. Stacie looked down Jessie's long, dirt road. She sighed and thought, "What if no one shows up?"

Just then she heard a car's horn honking in the driveway. Janet's mother pulled up. "I'm sorry," she called. "I took a wrong turn." She pointed behind her. "And everyone else was following me!"

A **caravan** of cars pulled into the driveway. Stacie's friends spilled out, shouting greetings and carrying presents.

Stacie hugged Skipper and then ran off to greet her friends.

They began by playing games. "Okay,

racers!" Jessie announced. "Get into your sacks!" Stacie and her friends climbed into their potato sacks. Most of them fell over. Giggling, they pulled themselves up and formed a starting line.

"On your mark!" Jessie paused. The racers leaned forward—then fell over again. They picked themselves up. "Get set!" Jessie called. "Go!"

Everyone cheered as the racers hopped away from the starting line. They swerved, bumped, and fell into one another. Jessie finally declared the race a tie because the racers were laughing too hard to finish.

Next, Jessie took some of Stacie's friends to the horse-riding area. She fitted everyone with a helmet. Then they took turns riding Whispy, Jessie's tan-and-white horse. Other kids went with Skipper to see the newly hatched chicks. The rest went with Barbie to milk some cows and feed a baby goat with a bottle.

By dinnertime everyone was ready for

Jessie's barbecued chicken and corn on the cob.

As it grew dark, Jessie and Skipper led Stacie and her friends out to a field near the creek. As they listened to the water trickling, the partygoers looked up at the night sky. Skipper pointed out the constellations, and Jessie set up a telescope. When a shooting star streaked across the sky, Stacie knew that she couldn't have asked for a better party.

Afterward, Barbie led everyone into the barn. "I hope you all left room for cake," she called. Stacie's friends admired the twinkling lights in the rafters. "This is Stacie's party," Barbie announced, "but she has a surprise for you. Close your eyes until we count to three."

Stacie, Skipper, Jessie, and Barbie each grabbed one of the ribbons hanging down from the balloon net. When they said *three,* they pulled the net away. Balloons drifted down as Skipper and Barbie tossed **confetti** everywhere.

HAPPY BIRTHDAY

BIRTHDAY

Kelly squealed with joy when a bright red balloon landed in her lap. Stacie's friends laughed as they batted the balloons at each other.

When all the balloons had settled, Jessie and Barbie carried in the cake. Stacie looked at it. *Happy Birthday, Stacie!* read the cake. A big candle shaped like a number nine shone brightly in the center.

"It's so beautiful!" exclaimed Stacie.

"Make a wish!" Skipper reminded her.

Todd called out, "Wish that my party will be as much fun as yours!"

Stacie was thrilled. She looked at Skipper and grinned. Then she blew out the candles. Barbie and Jessie sliced the cake. They set aside the first slice for Stacie. Then they handed out large pieces of cake to the others.

"Time for presents!" Skipper announced as she handed Stacie a present.

"Wait!" Stacie cried. She ran to a corner of

the barn and picked up three boxes she had hidden there. "First *I* have three presents to give." She handed one to Barbie, one to Skipper, and one to Kelly. "This is why I've been spending so much time in my room lately."

Barbie and Skipper looked puzzled. They opened their gifts. Stacie helped Kelly open hers. Inside each box was a framed picture of the four sisters. Stacie had decorated the frames herself. Each of them was different, but the words across the bottom were the same: *The Best Sisters Ever.*

"Oh, Stacie!" Barbie and Skipper cried.

"And this," Stacie exclaimed, "has been the best birthday party ever!"

"Hmmm," said Barbie with a twinkle in her eye. "Does that mean we shouldn't try to top it next year?"

"I didn't say that!" Stacie laughed. "But whatever it is," she said, hugging her sisters, "as long as we're together, I know it will be great!"